ANGELIQUE

BUFFALO
H U N T

CORA TAYLOR

the
Pettits

Aug 2002

ANGELIQUE

BUFFALO HUNT

CORA TAYLOR

Penguin Books

PENGUIN BOOKS

Published by the Penguin Group

Penguin Books Canada Ltd, 10 Alcorn Avenue, Toronto, Ontario, Canada M4V 3B2
Penguin Books Ltd, 80 Strand, London WC2R 0RL, England
Penguin Putnam Inc., 375 Hudson Street, New York, New York 10014, U.S.A.
Penguin Books Australia Ltd, 250 Camberwell Road, Camberwell, Victoria 3124, Australia
Penguin Books (NZ) Ltd, cnr Rosedale and Airborne Roads, Albany, Auckland 1310, New Zealand

Penguin Books Ltd, Registered Offices: Harmondsworth, Middlesex, England

DESIGN: MATTHEWS COMMUNICATIONS DESIGN INC.
MAP ILLUSTRATION: SHARON MATTHEWS
INTERIOR ILLUSTRATIONS: JAMES BENTLEY

First published, 2002

1   3   5   7   9   10   8   6   4   2

Copyright © Cora Taylor, 2002

The author wishes to thank The Canada Council for support to research and write this book. I
would like to thank the following people who helped with this book: Martina Purdon for
supplying me with all kinds of "buffalo hunt" lore; Dr. Nancy Gibson for the medical advice and
references to spruce gum; Dr. Jack Brink for digging up the pictures of the right beadwork (and
Martina again for sending them); Janice MacDonald for hunting down Metis pictures on the net;
and a big thank you to the late Victoria Callihoo who wrote down her memories of being on a
buffalo hunt when she was ten.

Manufactured in Canada

NATIONAL LIBRARY OF CANADA CATALOGUING IN PUBLICATION DATA

Taylor, Cora, 1936-
Angelique : buffalo hunt / Cora Taylor.

(Our Canadian girl)
ISBN 0-14-100271-9

1. Métis—Hunting—Juvenile fiction.   2. American bison hunting—Juvenile fiction.   3. Métis—
Juvenile fiction.
I. Title.   II. Series.

PS8589.A883A84   2002   jC813'.54   C2002-901219-8
PZ7.T21235An 2002

Visit Penguin Canada's website at **www.penguin.ca**

To my youngest grandchildren:
Adrienne Livingston, Alexander Mogg,
and Emily Thomas

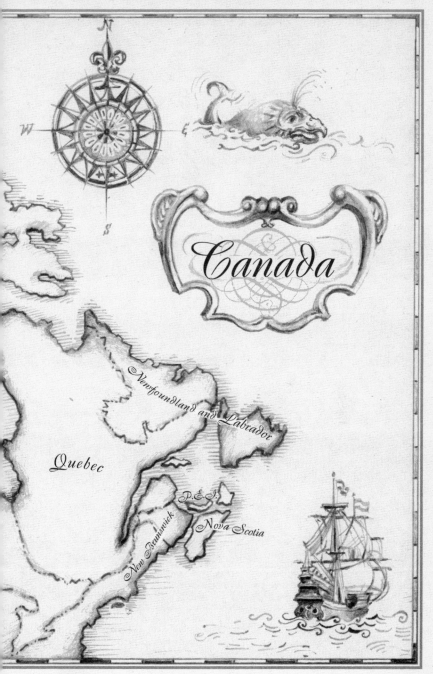

N

W

S

Canada

Newfoundland and Labrador

Quebec

P.E.I.

New Brunswick

Nova Scotia

 Marks the location of the story

MEET ANGELIQUE

A NGELIQUE DUMAS IS TEN YEARS OLD IN 1865. SHE and her family are Metis, which means that they are descended both from European fur traders and from the Cree, Ojibwa, and Saulteaux natives who had lived on the Canadian prairie for generations.

Angelique lives most of the year near Batoche in what is now northern Saskatchewan. Her father farms a small plot of land nearby, and sometimes the family travels to trade and buy goods at Fort Carlton. Angelique enjoys visiting friends in the small settlement and attends church there on Sundays and feast days, but her favourite time is when the families pack food and bedding in their Red River carts and head across the prairie in search of the great herds of prairie bison they call "buffalo."

The spring and fall hunts are necessary to the Metis. The meat from the buffalo provides food; sinew and bones become tools, and the hides are used for robes, tent covers, and moccasins. Utensils are made from the buffalo horns, hooves, and tails. Buffalo dung is used for fuel on the treeless plains. As well as providing for their own needs, the Metis are able to trade the hides and the pemmican they make for other things they require, such as blankets, pots, needles, tools, and fabric to be sewn into clothing.

This spring, Angelique is more excited than usual. At other hunts she has helped by fetching and carrying for her mother and the other women when they return from butchering the fallen buffalo. Sometimes she has helped to pound the dried meat for pemmican, and during the last fall hunt she picked berries to add to the pemmican. That was fun.

This year, for the first time, Angelique will join the older children who follow on foot after the horsemen. Their task is to look for the marker that the hunter throws down to identify the buffalo he has killed, so that the meat can be claimed by his family. It is an important job, and she is determined to do it well.

There is hard work on the hunt, but there is lots of fun, too. At night there will be dancing and songs around the fire. And instead of eating dried pemmican, they will feast on delicious meals from the best parts of the buffalo.

Times have been harder as the buffalo become more scarce. Angelique has heard that the women once carried back over three thousand buffalo tongues from one day's hunt. Now the herds are getting harder to find. Sometimes the women and children follow in the Red River carts for many miles before they catch up to the hunters.

Angelique's family is lucky in one way. Her father has been training a new horse, a "buffalo runner." Angelique adores the beautiful pinto named Michif, and she hopes that he will perform well and make them all proud on his first hunt.

So the beautiful springtime and the trip hold a mixture of feelings for Angelique: joy in the beauty and freedom of her people's life on the prairies, excitement that she is now truly a part of the hunt; and worry that she will not be able to do the new job that is expected of her. But that is not the worst part. She knows of the dangers of the hunt. And she knows that sometimes horses are gored, or hunters fall and are trampled. Will the hunt be a lucky one for her family this time?

CHAPTER N° 1

Always, the dream was the same. A dream of buffalo. One buffalo.

She would be walking. Walking towards a fallen bull buffalo as the hunt moved on ahead of her. She was alone, far ahead of the other women and children, eager to find her father's marker so she could run and tell her mother which buffalo was theirs to butcher. Too eager. She had come too soon.

As she neared the great animal it rose and came towards her. Not charging, but walking with great dignity.

And she could not run. She could only stand as if she were part of the prairie, rooted to the spot, like a tree or a stone—one of the great boulders that nestled into the earth. She stood and waited as the buffalo walked towards her.

And then, when it came so close she felt she would soon be near enough to touch the curling hair of its face or smell its grassy breath—then it stopped.

And still she could not run. Still she stood as if her moccasined feet had grown into the earth. As if held by the huge brown eyes that gazed into hers.

She was never afraid then. Just tired. Terribly tired, as if she'd been the one running from the hunters. So tired that when the great beast at last sighed and fell dead before her, she too fell. That was what awakened her. She moved to stop falling and jerked herself awake. She was trembling, her legs tangled in her blanket as though she'd been running in her sleep.

Now she lay curled in her blanket on the ground beside her little brother, Joseph. At least she hadn't wakened him. She knew that six-year-olds sometimes had trouble getting back to sleep, or even lying still enough to let others dream. Ten-year-olds knew better.

Angelique inched away from the warm space where their blankets touched. She could see well enough now to make out the sleeping form of her mother across from her. Papa was gone, though.

As she slipped noiselessly out of the tipi into the early-morning mist she could see the men mounting their horses and riding off. The scouting party, five men, was leaving. Her father, Louie, would be with them. She watched the silhouette of horses and riders against the pale dawn sky.

Yesterday the scouts had not returned until late in the day. They had seen no buffalo. Not one.

It had been three days since Angelique and her family had left Batoche. Along the way, other families had joined them, until nearly a hundred carts were strung out across the prairie. Three days of bumping along in creaking Red River carts, hoping for a herd. They hadn't expected anything on their first day out, but over the next day and the next, people had become quieter, more expectant.

The spring hunt was important. More important this year, since last fall's hunt had gone badly. Winter had come early and the great herds had moved south too soon. Not as many buffalo had been killed, and there had been only enough pemmican for their own use. Selling the pemmican the women made was vital if they were to buy the things they needed from the fort—tea, sugar and molasses, pots and kettles. Sometimes there would even be enough credit left for something special. Angelique remembered the shiny blue cloth she'd seen last time they were there. She could imagine her mother sewing it into a blouse for her, a beautiful satin blouse for church and parties. She could almost feel its smoothness on her cheek. This *had* to be a good hunt.

But the dream haunted her. She hoped it was a sign that there would be buffalo today. It *had* to mean that. Or perhaps it was just that her excitement about this special hunt had crept into her mind as she slept. This year she had a big part to play. For the first time she would run after the hunt. She hoped it was just that. She would not let herself think that it was worry about her father, or her beloved Michif.

She moved quietly. Moccasined feet are silent. How else had her father moved away from his family so early without waking them?

Angelique loved this time of day. The prairie lay peaceful and silent and the air smelled fresh and new. They were camped in a small hollow not far from a hill. She would climb that hill and watch the day dawn.

They were not supposed to leave camp, but surely her mother wouldn't mind. After all, she wasn't really leaving, she would stay in sight. Close enough to run back. *I'll be back before anyone wakes up anyway,* she told herself.

Other years, François would have been with her. They would have climbed the hill together. François LaVallée was ten too. She'd known him for years. They'd been playmates on earlier hunts. But last year François had started doing boy things. And she'd been stuck behind, helping hang the strips of meat to dry for pemmican, keeping the fires going, learning to cook and do beadwork. It wasn't fair. The boys got to have traplines in winter, and they rode about practising firing their imaginary guns while galloping their horses. They had to learn to load the guns. Some of them would ride with powder horns and shot bags across their shoulders, even before they were old enough for guns. She wasn't sure if she was angry or sad about the way François had changed, but she missed him. The LaVallées had joined the hunt two days ago, and François hadn't even said hello.

He didn't know that this year Angelique would be doing a boy's job. She'd been on hunts before, but then she'd stayed behind with the carts and the other children and had come along only as the women came to cut and hang the meat.

This year she would be running ahead of the women and children to search among the fallen buffalo for her father's marker. Usually he would throw one of his gauntlets, a beaded glove, beside the animal he had killed. All of the men did that. It was the beadwork that identified it. Angelique would be looking for her mother's distinctive wild rose pattern, the same that was on her own moccasins.

She was almost to the top now. Her moccasins felt damp from the dewy grass, and already the sky was lightening. Streaks of pale gold and pink coloured the eastern horizon. Away from the camp and the resting horses and people, the air was filled only with the smell of the grasses she had trampled as she'd walked: wild thyme and sage mixed with the scent of faraway streams and trees and the little lakes that came only in spring. She breathed it blissfully.

Later, the day would be filled with dust and screeching from the carts as the Metis hunters and their families moved along. Now the silence was broken only by birds. Angelique smiled. She always thought they sounded sleepy this early in the morning, their first chirps and warbles muted as if they were clearing their throats. A killdeer appeared from nowhere, almost at her feet. It cried its name softly as it moved with its smooth run to disappear into the tall grasses as quickly as it had appeared.

Horses and riders—she heard them before she saw them. They were coming her way, but it was a long moment before they appeared over the crest of the hill opposite the one on which she stood. Why were the scouts returning so soon?

Angelique turned and ran back to camp.

CHAPTER N°2

If she'd meant to sound an alarm, she was too late. Already the camp was moving about excitedly, with people pausing to look at the riders as they drew near. They were close enough for Angelique to recognize the men riding in front.

There was her father riding his special horse, Michif.

"Buffalo!" someone cried, and the word echoed through the camp. It seemed to change the day. The calm morning became charged with anticipation. Movement picked up: the women's breakfast preparations around the campfires became brisker; even the toddlers sensed something in the air and began to dash about.

"A big herd . . ." The news spread. Men hurried to get their flintlocks or muskets.

Angelique ran too. She caught the reins of her father's horse as he rode into the camp. "I'll take him." She smiled. "Maman has some bannock ready." She knew the hunters would be leaving soon.

She rubbed her hand along the horse's sweaty flank. She'd take him out a bit before she put him back on the tether. A little distance away from camp the prairie grass was long and there was new green beneath. Michif could eat while she used the dry grass to rub the sweat from his coat.

"You spoil that horse," her mother always said.

But Angelique had been there with her father when he'd first seen the foal and named it. He'd laughed at the great pinto patches on the tiny animal, the blobs of white and bay all over his

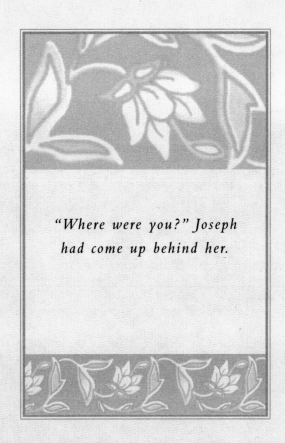

*"Where were you?" Joseph
had come up behind her.*

body. "You're a mixture," he'd said, "like our talk. Some French, some Cree, a little Saulteaux. You're Michif."

The horse was nearly four years old now and one of the fastest in their settlement. This would be his first hunt. Papa said he had the makings of a fine buffalo runner.

Angelique rubbed the quickly drying sweat streaks away. "Run well, good Michif," she whispered. The horse lifted his head from grazing and rubbed his muzzle along her side, gently at first, then pushing so much she nearly toppled. She didn't care, she just laughed and pushed back. It was Michif's way of showing affection.

"Where were you?" Joseph had come up behind her, and now he was shooting her an angry look. "You were gone when I woke up! I looked and looked. You're not supposed to leave camp. I'll tell Maman."

Angelique stared at him. He hadn't seen her running back, had he? She decided to distract him.

"It's good that you are here," she said. "You can help me take Michif to the tethering place. Papa will need him soon." She tugged the horse away from his grazing and handed the lead to her brother.

It worked. Joseph eagerly took the reins and began to walk. Angelique felt relief, but Joseph was not letting her off so easily. Halfway there he turned.

"Maybe I could ride and you could lead?"

Angelique sighed. Why must he be so difficult? It was not a problem of riding. Every six-year-old could ride, and Joseph was even better than most.

"Joseph, you know very well that if Michif is to be a good buffalo runner, no one must ride him but Papa. He is being trained."

Joseph sighed and kept walking.

Angelique made sure that he'd made a proper knot when he tethered Michif. It had to hold the horse but be tied so that her father could release it with just one tug of the end of the rope.

"So where were you?" Joseph persisted as they walked back to their own tipi.

Angelique sighed and rolled her eyes at him. That was a mistake.

"Where were you, Buffalo Eyes?" he teased, dancing out of reach. He knew that she hated his nickname for her. At least now she could chase him and make him forget his questions. And they were off, racing through camp, dodging other children. Angelique was sure that she could have caught him, but she also knew she'd better get back and help her mother. She let him go as he dodged off between the Red River carts.

"Buffalo Eyes!" he yelled again as she turned away.

A stupid nickname. So what if her eyes were large and brown, and maybe they *were* the colour of the buffalo. Suddenly she remembered the eyes of the dying buffalo in her dream.

CHAPTER N.º 3

In camp, the women hurried to prepare the morning meal. On other mornings fires were not kindled so quickly. Everyone played a waiting game: which family would be the first to have a fire? Then the others would send a youngster with a stick to bring back the flame. Nobody wanted to spend the time striking a flint and nursing the spark in the birch punk that everyone carried. Easier to wait and watch for the smoke of the first fire.

Yesterday it had been their fire that everyone

had borrowed. Maman was teaching her to use the flint. It wasn't easy. You had to hit it just right, and if you didn't hold it properly it was your finger that got hit, not the stone. There was a knack to holding it close enough and aiming so that the spark flew right into the dry fluff that came from the inside of a dead birch tree. Of course, if you did everything right it worked like magic. A spark, a tiny flame, and soon a lovely campfire. Yesterday she had done everything right.

Today there was no waiting for another's fire. There wasn't time to wait, the hunters must be fed. Everyone was eager to go. Her mother had not complained of her absence. Good. That meant that Joseph hadn't told on her.

Her father had already eaten and was turning back with the other men. Horses snorted and pranced, sensing the excitement, eager to be off.

It seemed the herd was a good-sized one. Hundreds of buffalo. Maman had told her that when she was Angelique's age there were huge herds, thousands of buffalo, but the herds had been getting smaller every year.

"Look out, Buffalo Eyes!" Joseph was back, giving her a shove as he pushed past her to the fire. He gave her an impish look as he tore a piece of bannock from the pan her mother had placed on a flat stone by the campfire. It was last night's bannock, but warm from the fire it was still good.

Angelique smiled sweetly at her brother. She wouldn't let him bother her with his teasing. She really felt a little sorry for him. Usually it was the boys who got to be first to go among the fallen buffalo, but she was the eldest in their family, and Papa had said Joseph was too young. Today, while he stayed behind, she would be the grown-up one. She could be generous and ignore his taunts.

Besides, nothing annoyed him more than being ignored.

The hunters were gathered near the ridge of the hill where Angelique had stood earlier. The hunt was very organized, like an army. And very strict. Anyone who disobeyed the lieutenant's

orders would be sent away. This hunt had nearly
a hundred men, which was why the camp was
so large.

Angelique watched as the leader, Monsieur
Dumont, rode among the men giving instructions. They would be planning their approach.
The last thing they would wish to do was stampede the herd the wrong way, especially with the
families camped so close by. On the other hand,
it would be good to do the killing nearby so that
the women did not have to travel too far to
butcher. This was a good camping place, close to
water. It would be much easier if they didn't have
to move camp tonight.

The older boys who were still too young to
ride in the hunt had moved up, ready to follow.
They were doing the same job as Angelique. She
moved over to stand with them. Some of the
boys glanced towards her and turned away,
looking superior. There was only one other girl.
Angelique recognized Marie Letendre. Marie was
the eldest in her family now. Last winter her

brother had fallen through the ice on the lake and drowned. Marie did not look happy to be there.

Angelique did not know Marie very well, even though she saw her each year at the hunt. The Letendres were among the families from other communities who joined the hunt every day as they travelled. Now there were nearly a hundred families. A hundred Red River carts. No wonder there was so much noise and dust as they moved along. It was a wonder that any buffalo came near them.

Angelique realized nervously that she was probably the youngest there. Except for François. To her surprise, François turned now and waved to her, though he stayed with the bigger boys.

The riders left. They would move slowly until they were close to the herd again. That way they saved their horses' strength and did not startle the herd into running too soon.

Angelique and the others waited. They would have set off immediately—after all, they were on foot and eager to go—but they had a leader too. Jean Laframboise had been injured in a buffalo hunt years before. He walked with a limp and one of his arms had not mended properly. He could still ride well, but shooting, especially the business of using both hands to reload, was impossible for him.

Angelique hoped that she would be able to see at least some of the hunt itself, though she knew that would be very unlikely. The dust from the hooves of five or six hundred buffalo would make it impossible. Still, she wanted to see the herd begin to move. So she stood there aching with anticipation. "Please, please go," she whispered to herself.

As if he had heard, Jean gave the signal and they began to move along the ridge following the hunters.

CHAPTER N.º 4

The older boys fell in behind Jean right away. Then they had to slow down so they wouldn't pass him. And that was when Angelique realized that being smaller just might be an advantage.

She and François were moving steadily towards the front, slipping through between the older boys. Sometimes they would give her a dirty look, but they couldn't do much more. If Jean saw them pushing or shoving anyone they would be sent back to camp and have to wait and come back when the women followed. No one wanted to risk that disgrace.

They moved up quickly. Occasionally Angelique would catch sight of François and they would exchange happy grins. They reached the hill where she had first seen the scouting party that morning. By now the two youngest were in the lead with Jean, and they were there to see the herd on the distant plain, a huge black blanket spread across the prairie. It was certainly the biggest herd that she had ever seen.

And now she could see the hunters moving in, like a fan, towards the herd. She thought for a moment she could make out Michif racing along the edge. It was his first buffalo hunt. And in a way, it was hers, too.

Now the buffalo began to move, slowly at first, then shifting from a trot to a gallop. She could make out a few stragglers along the edge, but mostly what she saw was a black mass starting to flow across the plain. From where she stood it looked like molasses spilling. Then the dust rose in clouds, and a sound, like the distant rumble of thunder, came back to her.

She thought she saw Michif following close to one of the buffalo at the edge of the herd, saw the buffalo fall. If that was really her father, then he had claimed the first kill. It would be easy for her to find.

Jean was leading them down towards the plain, and a runner was sent back to camp. The women would soon come with the carts, and the process of butchering would begin.

Now everyone was running. Jean knew that by the time they arrived the hunters would be gone, so he no longer held them back. Even though the teenaged boys had longer legs and the faster runners began to outdistance her, she didn't care. She loved running. She and François used to race just for the joy of it. He might sometimes beat her in a race, but he could never catch her.

Her full skirt was catching on her legs so she hiked it up with both hands. Maman was not there to see and lecture her about modesty. And everyone was running too fast to notice or care.

Angelique put her head down and flew. She was careful to watch for hummocks and gopher holes and buffalo dung so that she could skim around or over them. A wonderful feeling— flying—free.

Some of the others were falling behind but Angelique only dodged around them and kept on. She felt as if she could run for miles. She wasn't the least bit tired.

Then she saw the first buffalo ahead of her—a great brown-black heap on the prairie. There were more farther ahead. Lying still, like boulders.

Angelique slowed, remembering her dream. But these buffalo were on their sides, motionless. Dead.

She checked the first one, a young bull. A deerhide glove lay beside him, but the embroidery was not her mother's. Now she moved on, running slowly.

The other runners had moved on, checking the buffalo. One or two had found their family mark. And now she could hear the carts coming behind, and when she turned she could see the cloud of dust showing that they were on their way.

Angelique and François arrived at another fallen animal. François looked at her and smiled. "Good run!" he said.

They beamed at each other. They had shown the older ones. And they stood a minute, proud of each other, like the friends they used to be.

This buffalo belonged to neither of them. They moved on, checking together. She remembered where she'd seen her father, on the northern edge of the herd.

The uneasiness she had felt earlier—that a buffalo might rise up as it did in her dream— came back to her, but it was forgotten in a moment when her eyes spotted the familiar gauntlet lying beside a cow buffalo. She was tempted to run ahead with François and try to

Her eyes spotted the familiar gauntlet lying beside a cow buffalo.

find another kill, but now she had to wait for her mother to come.

If only Joseph were there. Everyone in the camp was coming now, and he was a good runner. Not as good as she was, of course. But at least he wouldn't be as slow as the carts.

At last she saw him. He really was fast. She waved the gauntlet and jumped up and down, watching as he veered away from the other running children and dashed towards her.

CHAPTER N.º 5

"I saw it, Joseph!" Angelique felt sorry that her brother had missed the run. But perhaps if she shared her part in the hunt, he would feel as if he had been there too.

"I saw, in the very beginning, when the herd began to move . . . I saw Michif coming up beside the buffalo. *This* buffalo! I saw Papa make the kill!"

It was a good kill. She could see that the shot had entered exactly in the right place—behind the foreleg. If you drew a line from the knee, it was only the length of her little finger higher.

The animal would have been dead before it hit the ground. Her father was a wonderful shot. Buffalo hunters had to be, to be able to fire with such accuracy from a galloping horse.

Joseph beamed. "Michif has the courage." They smiled at each other.

There were four qualities a buffalo runner had to have. Now Joseph was counting them off on his fingers. "A buffalo runner must be able to run at top speed over a long distance; he must be intelligent and respond to commands; he must be able to move quickly and turn and race over uneven ground without stumbling; *and* he must have courage!"

Angelique wanted to hug him. Joseph was as excited as she was. Many horses possessed the first three qualities, but those same horses might then fear the buffalo when they got too near, shying away and sometimes even throwing their riders under the galloping feet of the herd.

Michif had passed the test today. He was a proven buffalo runner and that made him one of the family's most valuable possessions. Michif would never be sold or traded away now, Angelique thought happily.

"Angelique? Why do you stay here?" Joseph was poking her. "You should see if Papa was able to reload and shoot another. I will stay with this one until Maman comes."

She did hug him then. He really was a most excellent little brother, she decided as she turned and started to race away.

She almost laughed when she heard him call out behind her.

"You call *that* running? Buffalo Eyes!"

Angelique didn't bother to look at any of the fallen animals until she'd run a good distance. It would have taken a while for her father to prepare to take another shot. He would have had to reload, and that meant holding the reins in his teeth and using both hands. Not an easy task. Another reason why a buffalo runner had to be sure-footed.

She spotted another gauntlet lying beside an animal ahead of her. It looked like the familiar pink beadwork. It was! Another cow—that was wonderful. Cows had better meat, but they were also harder to kill.

She'd heard the men talk. Her father and the others would sit around and tell their tales of the hunt, while she and the women brought them food. They said the cows were faster than the bulls, so once the herd was at full run they would end up leading. The calves would struggle to keep up, but the hunters never killed them. Nobody liked veal. Unless they were very young, they would survive with the herd after the run was over.

She looked up to see her father and some of the other hunters riding back. Two kills were all anyone could hope for on a hunt. And two animals were all the family needed for now. There would be feasting tonight, but before that there was much work to be done.

Michif came toward her. Did he look different now that he was a prized buffalo runner? He was the same to her. She had always prized him. She ran forward and caught the reins from her father.

"Good Michif!" she sang, "my brave one!" She would give him such a rubdown to remove the streaks of sweat still dripping from his flanks. But first a walk to cool him off before Maman arrived and put her to work.

CHAPTER N.º 6

Now the work began. Her mother brought two long skinning knives from the cart. Angelique watched her make the initial cuts and begin to slice away the hide. Grim-faced, Angelique forced herself to grip the bloody hide and help her mother pull it back, but the weight of it was too much. Soon her father came and took her place.

She helped as he pegged the hide out to dry. Hides were used for sleeping robes, or tanned and used for moccasins, or sewn together to make the tipis that the Metis used when travelling on the hunt. As well, they could be traded at the fort for supplies. This one, though, would probably be sewn into a bag to hold the pemmican later on.

Angelique brushed her hair out of her eyes. Already, sweat was trickling down her neck. The beautiful day was hot now. She looked sadly into the distance. The herd and hunters had gone, and she wished she could be with them.

"Angelique! *Ashtum vite! Dépêche-toi!*" Her mother was telling her to hurry. There would be no standing around staring into space. "Come and prepare the drying racks!"

Swiftly she brought the willow sticks from the cart. In no time she had built a drying rack for the strips of meat. Three sticks in tipi form tied with a thong, a long stick balanced across the top of two tipis, and it was done.

Just in time, too. Joseph was already bringing first strips her mother had cut. Together they back and forth, hanging the meat.

36

Angelique was grateful that a breeze had sprung up. Still, flies had begun to gather, attracted by the fresh meat.

"Joseph," she commanded, hoping that in the excitement of the work he'd forget that he usually argued with any order she gave, "see if you can find some buffalo chips, while I build the smudge fire."

They'd been working steadily, and both were hot and tired, but there was still much to do.

For a moment it looked as though Joseph was going to rebel. He gave her an angry look, as if to say, "Who are you to tell me what to do?" But then, as she'd hoped, he broke into an impish grin and ran to the cart to get a sack.

"I'll be back before you have the fire lit!" he yelled.

Angelique smiled. *No chance,* she thought. She'd already noticed that the Larocque family, who were skinning a buffalo nearby, had a fire lit. She would just borrow a light.

First she needed some dried grass, though, and she would have to run a distance to get it, because the grasses nearby had been trampled in the stampede.

She left quickly. Lovely to be running again and not working. Nice not to be lifting bloody strips of meat, brushing away flies, and wishing she were somewhere else.

Once on the hillside, where there were tufts of dried grass, she was almost sorry she'd come. She knew she would never want to leave. Away from the smell of the butchering the air was fresh, and she could hear the sound of a meadowlark and see the yellow splash of colour where the buffalo beans grew.

Worse than that, she could see her fellow runners, the older boys she'd outdistanced when they'd run to the hunt. Their job was to patrol the area around the fallen buffalo to keep away the prairie wolves that would be attracted by the scent of a fresh kill. Many of them carried old flintlocks or muskets, looking very full of themselves. François had joined them. Angelique sniffed. She had a good notion to go over and lecture him on the sin of Pride.

"There probably isn't a wolf for miles," she mumbled as she ran back to get the fire started and catch up hanging the strips of meat that her mother had piled up during her absence.

She was angry with François. She knew it wasn't his fault that he got a better job than she did, but that just made her more annoyed. *It's not fair,* she thought as she headed back to camp with her kindling grass.

Joseph was back before her. She couldn't believe it but there he was, a half-filled bag of buffalo chips over his shoulder. That didn't improve her mood.

"You didn't get enough!" she scolded. "Why didn't you fill the bag? You'll just have to go again!"

She'd picked up a glowing stick from the Larocque campfire on her way. Once she had shoved it into the ball of dry prairie wool she'd gathered, she only had to blow on it to get a blaze.

"I'll tend the smudge," Joseph offered. "You can go for the chips."

Angelique's mood changed instantly. Gathering the flat, sun-baked pies of buffalo dung they called buffalo chips was really children's work, but you got to be away, alone on the prairie. And on this beautiful day she could think of nothing better.

CHAPTER N°7

All work stopped as a cloud of dust rose up over the ridge nearby, and people strained their eyes as Monsieur Dumont and several other men rode along. A riderless horse was with them. It must have belonged to someone who'd still been following the herd, trying to make a kill. François came running towards the silent group of women who had gathered to watch.

"It is Jacques Letendre," François panted. "His horse stepped in a gopher hole . . . he was thrown under the feet of the buffalo. He has

41

been trampled and dragged." He stopped and stood a moment to catch his breath. "I am supposed to find his wife and his daughter. Do you know where Marie is?"

Angelique shook her head. When had she last seen Marie? At the beginning of the run?

"Maman?" She knew her job was to help her mother, but maybe this was more important. "I could help François look . . ."

Her mother nodded. "Poor Madame Letendre . . ." she sighed as she returned to her work. "Her son, and now her husband."

It was not until they'd run another half mile among the fallen buffalo that Angelique found Marie. Her mother had already gone with their Red River cart to help bring her father back to camp. Angelique could think of nothing to say to comfort the older girl. François did better.

"They will bring your father to my *kokum*. Do you want to come with us and wait for him there?"

Angelique had forgotten that François's grand-
mother was the daughter of a Cree medicine
woman. She saw the look of relief on Marie's
face. The three of them set out to return to camp.

No one spoke. They saved their breath for
running.

It was some time before the cart carrying
Marie's father arrived. Angelique stayed with Marie,
although, aside from bringing her a cup of hot,
sweet tea, there seemed to be nothing she could
do. Marie sat and stared into space, and Angelique
could only do the same. Until they knew what
the man's injuries were, it was useless to speak of
the results. The buffalo in her dream had fallen
dead. Perhaps that had been a sign that someone
would die in the hunt.

Marie heard the cart before anyone else. She leapt up and began to run towards the sound. She had not just been staring into space, Angelique realized. She had been listening.

Angelique knew there was no reason now for her to stay. She should be going back to help her mother, she thought guiltily. But François was still here. Maybe, if she waited, they could go back to the butchering together.

The injured man lay on a pile of bloody blankets, and the hunters lifted him carefully from the cart and carried him to lie in front of the medicine woman's tipi. Angelique was relieved to see that, although he was moaning and in obvious pain, he was still alive. She watched as Marie and her mother made way for François's *kokum* to examine the injuries. Soon the old woman was busily smearing something on the wounds. Almost clear, it looked too sticky to spread.

It did not appear that the man had been gored, but his legs seemed badly injured. His deerhide pants were torn, tattered by the hooves that had passed over him.

For what seemed a very long time, Angelique watched and waited. Eventually, slowly, the old woman rose. She looked past Madame Letendre and saw Angelique and François.

"Shouldn't you two young ones be helping your mothers?" she said sternly. Then her wrinkled old face softened. "You may tell the others that he is not as badly hurt as he might have been. Now go!"

François didn't hesitate. He began to run.

Angelique turned to Marie. "If there is anything . . ." It was all she could think of. Again she felt useless, but there was a ghost of a smile from Marie. "Thank you," she said.

That night, Angelique pulled a buffalo robe out of the tipi to lie under the stars. She'd eaten so much her stomach felt full up to her chin, but the fresh buffalo meat had been such a treat. Everyone had feasted on the choicest pieces, the roasted hump and boiled tongue. No more pemmican stew for them for a while.

Joseph had barely curled up in his blanket on the robe before he was asleep, but she sat up a while to listen to the music. Jean Laframboise had brought his fiddle and had soon begun the Red River Reel.

At first people had stood about, anxiously discussing the accident, but soon a few began to dance. Jean would recover, perhaps even be able to ride and hunt the buffalo again. Life was hard, the hunt was dangerous, and people knew that they must celebrate when they could.

Angelique fought to keep her eyes open as the couples whirled about the campfire, the flickering light glancing off the bright fabric of the women's blouses and the men's shirts. The men's red *voyageur* sashes made splashes of colour that seemed to glow and run together.

She gave up and lay down, staring up at the night sky. The last thing she saw were the millions of stars that seemed to be falling down around her. *Once,* she thought, sleepily, *the buffalo were like that.*

CHAPTER № 8

Morning came very early on the prairie, but today Angelique did not waken at dawn. There had been no dream to wake her; even so, it was not a good awakening.

A fly walked across her nose. She brushed it away sleepily. No luck, it was back on her cheek. She slapped, angry now, and hurt herself enough that she was now thoroughly awake and sitting up. It hadn't been a fly at all.

"Joseph!" What a pest that boy was. She sprang up and was after him so fast he dropped the bit of foxtail grass he'd been using to tickle her face.

"Maman says you are to get up!"

He was laughing so hard she could easily have caught him, but the sun was already over the horizon, so she turned back to their camp.

Her mother was gathering up a few sticks and a pot, getting ready to go back to the remains of the buffalo.

"Eat!" she said, gesturing towards the covered cast-iron pot by the fire. "Then come and help me."

Angelique nodded. The leftover stew wasn't very warm but it was good. She ladled some meat onto a piece of bannock and folded it over.

Today would be much easier. The main work had been done yesterday. Both cows had been skinned and cut up; the hanging meat would be drying nicely. Today they would mostly be watching the smudge fires—a job for Joseph and herself.

She wondered at her mother's strength. She'd worked very hard yesterday with the butchering and preparing food, and she'd still had energy for dancing. The men, too, should have been tired from the hard riding and hauling meat, but watching them last night you'd never have known.

Angelique supposed it was the feeling of celebration. A good hunt, good food and plenty of it, hides and pemmican to sell at the fort. And, probably best of all, Monsieur Letendre, though badly hurt, would be all right. Not every hunt was as lucky.

Tomorrow, the scouts would be checking to see if the herd was still close enough and had settled down enough to do another run. Angelique's family had their two buffalo, more than the cart could carry. Extra meat would be given away. This time, her father would be riding to kill a buffalo for another man. Someone like Jean Laframboise, who could not hunt for his own family. Or Marie's father. More work. More feasting and celebration.

After finishing her breakfast, Angelique, instead of taking the direct route downhill to her mother, decided to say "Good day" to Michif.

He nickered softly in reply as she came up and began to stroke him.

"Why don't you give him a drink, while you are here?" her father called to her. "I'll tell Maman where you are. When he's finished, leave him tethered. I'll need him for the hunt."

Angelique beamed her thanks. There was nothing she'd rather do than spend some time just enjoying the day and being with Michif.

She picked her way along the track to the muddy banks of the small stream they had camped beside. It was nothing like the clear water it had been when they came. Hoof marks everywhere. Moving upstream, she finally found a clear place, and she sat by a clump of wolf willow holding Michif's halter shank as he drank.

This was perfect. The freshness of the day, the amazing feeling of space with the huge sky above her. A feeling of peace and freedom that she loved.

"Good day!"

Angelique jumped guiltily and looked around. It was only François. His moccasins had brought him close without a sound. She knew he'd crept up behind her on purpose. They used to practise stalking each other. She laughed. It was good to see him. Especially as she noticed that he already carried the sack for chips.

"Wait!" she said. "I'll come gathering with you!"

Now she could delay going back even longer. She could share François's sack. If she arrived with half a sack of buffalo chips, Maman could not be angry that it had taken her a little longer. Besides, she had Papa's permission to water Michif.

"Good!" François looked grateful, and Angelique felt a little guilty.

Angelique shook the lead. "Hurry, Michif!"

Obediently the horse raised his dripping muzzle from the water and came to her.

Angelique couldn't help the feeling of pride that burst in her chest. Here was a prize horse, a noble buffalo runner proven in the hunt, obeying her. In front of François. The day could not be better.

Several other children were out dragging half-filled sacks behind them. The flat plates of dried dung were getting harder to find now that so many were looking.

"Joseph! What are you doing here?"

The answer to Angelique's question was fairly obvious. Like the others, he was dragging a sack.

"Maman said I could come!"

He sounded more hurt than defiant, and Angelique instantly regretted her annoyance.

Before they knew it they'd travelled quite a distance from the others. Angelique was tempted to pick a bouquet of buffalo beans for her mother—the yellow flowers were so cheerful—but there would be no place to put them.

"Look!" François had run ahead to a little rise and was pointing. "It's the herd!"

Joseph ran to stand beside him. "It's so close!" There was excitement in his voice—and fear.

Angelique was torn. She knew the smart thing would be to turn and hurry back. She looked behind her. There was not another child to be seen. Had they come that far?

The boys had dropped to the ground so that they wouldn't attract the herd's attention. "Come and see!"

Excitement won over fear. Angelique got down on her hands and knees and crawled to the hill. There was a boulder on the rise that they could hide behind. Noiselessly, the three crept towards it.

There were buffalo everywhere. Angelique had never seen them so close. Not living ones. Except in the dream. And remembering the dream, she was afraid.

She grabbed François's arm and tried to pull him back. It was all she could do to keep herself from leaping up and running as fast as she could. Back. Away.

The herd was spread out below them; some were even feeding on the slope close by.

We must be downwind from them, Angelique thought. *We're lucky.*

François had shaken her hand off. He seemed content just to lie there, watching. Now Angelique grabbed Joseph and tried to pull him away. At first he resisted; he turned angrily towards her. But then, perhaps recognizing the look of determination on her face, he gave in. She hung on and pulled as she backed away, crouching so as not to alarm the herd. With a look of disgust, Joseph followed, and at last François came too.

As soon as they were able to stand up, out of sight of the herd, Angelique took off at top speed. She didn't wait to hear what François would say, she was running flat out, away from the herd.

At least she thought she was running away from the herd.

CHAPTER N° 9

There were more boulders than she remembered, although she could still see buffalo beans blooming. She slowed. Surely she'd have remembered the boulders—especially that big dark one.

François caught up to her then. His turn to grab her arm, so hard it hurt.

"Are you a fool?" he said, giving her a shake. "This is not the way."

Angelique was staring at the dark boulder partly hidden by the other grey and pinkish stones ahead. Had it moved? No. Surely it was her imagination.

She turned to François. "I . . . I . . . thought it was the way . . . I just wanted to get Joseph away. We were too close to the herd."

François was pointing. "Look!"

Angelique turned. She could see the hunters' horses coming over the rise. They stood for a moment. There was Papa on Michif, and she could see Monsieur Dumont moving among them, giving instructions for the hunt.

"Now we are in big trouble!" François was pushing her away. "We are not supposed to be here!"

Angelique knew that in a moment the riders would be coming their way and they would be seen.

"Quick! Hide!" François was already dashing towards the boulders, with Joseph close behind.

This time, as Angelique turned to follow, she was sure the big brown boulder moved.

"François!" she screamed. There was no chance

of them hiding now. She had to warn him.

The brown boulder stood: a buffalo cow, blood oozing from her side, head down, swaying a little.

François had seen it too and veered away, still running, but Joseph stopped as if turned to stone. Instead of running towards the horsemen as François had, he stood.

Angelique stood too. Her legs wouldn't move—just as in the dream. But this was a cow, not a bull, and it was moving now. Not in the sedate walk of her dream but starting to run, tail up, beginning its charge straight towards Joseph.

The paralysis left her then. There was no time to scream. She ran towards Joseph and her body struck him at full speed, knocking him flat. She did not slow. She ran faster than she had ever run before, crossing in front of the cow.

Two riders were coming towards her. Michif was the faster horse. But the buffalo was so close.

And then she was swept up so fast it felt like flying. The pounding hooves, the feel of her

*And then she was swept up so
fast it felt like flying.*

father's arms, the angry grunt of the buffalo cow in pursuit. But the cow couldn't catch Michif. He was fast as the wind.

A shot rang out, and she looked back. François's father, riding behind them, had fired true. The cow fell, dead.

She saw François move now. Jumping up to be caught, safe, riding behind his father, who leaned down and scooped Joseph up in front.

The other riders had gone after the herd. She could see it begin to move, the way it had yesterday, flowing across the plain.

They rode in silence. At last her father spoke.

"It's good that you had the sack. People will know that you were only gathering chips and wandered too far."

Relief filled Angelique so that she could hardly speak. "We saw the herd and then I ran . . . I thought I was running back. . . ."

"Well, François's family will have the cow. She had been wounded. She would have died there otherwise."

Angelique was grateful for her father's kindness. "I am so lucky that you were there, and that Michif is so fast."

"Yes." Her father's voice seemed very sad.

It is because I have made him miss the hunt, she thought. She felt dreadfully unhappy.

It was not until they were back at camp and she slid down from Michif that she noticed the blood on her hands. Then, with a terrible shock, she realized what had happened.

CHAPTER N.º 10

Angelique could hardly speak. She could not look at Michif. Tears stung her eyes.

"Oh, Papa . . ." She held her bloody hand up for him to see. She couldn't say any more.

Her father looked down at her and nodded, his eyes sad.

He'd known. How could she not have known it too? Michif had galloped in like a good buffalo runner beside the cow when her father had grabbed her. But buffalo cows are quick, and even this wounded one had been able to turn and gore.

"Michif." She put her head against his chest, sobbing soundlessly, smelling the sharp scent of his sweat. Horses who had been gored were no good as buffalo runners. They lost courage. That is, if they lived. Most did not.

But Michif had run on. Perhaps he was not hurt too badly. He would live. He *had* to live.

Her father had dismounted and was checking Michif. Angelique forced herself to look.

There was so much blood. Blood on his flank and rump. It was hard to tell where the wound was. Already flies were buzzing around Michif's bloody side.

Her father turned silently and was leading Michif back to the stream. Angelique followed. He stopped and led the horse into the clear water. Chest deep, with the water nearly covering Michif's tail, he began gently to wash away the blood.

Angelique wanted to be there, to help, but she could only stand on the bank and watch, weeping quietly. She watched as the water around Michif turned red. She hardly noticed François silently sit down beside her.

"It can't be in the belly," François said softly, "or your father would not have taken him so deep in the water."

Angelique felt a tickle of hope. She hadn't thought of that. She turned and smiled at François through her tears. She knew belly wounds were fatal. A hunter would shoot his buffalo runner rather than let it suffer that death.

Michif would live. He had to. And more than anything he had to run again. Beyond that, Angelique dared not hope.

Her father was leading Michif out of the water. The blood gone, she could see the wound now, an ugly gouge on the horse's rump. Flies had already begun to buzz around it.

Her father looked at her. "It should heal, if there is no infection. Michif will have a big scar, though." His smile was still sad. Angelique did not dare ask if he would ever be a buffalo runner again. She knew only time would tell.

Angelique followed behind her father, walking beside Michif, waving her hand above his wound to keep the flies away. She tried to ignore the limp he had. Maybe it was her imagination. When they reached the tethering place, she stayed.

Swish! The coarse hair of Michif's tail hair caught her across the face, stinging her cheeks, as he tried to rid himself of the flies.

"Michif!" she yelped. The horse looked back at her, nickering gently. Laughing a little, she was at his head in a moment, rubbing her cheek against his. "You must get better so that you can forgive me for causing this. My fault." Tears welled in her eyes again. Michif pushed at her with his muzzle as if nothing had changed.

François appeared again, waving a severed buffalo tail, the end like a whisk. "To keep the flies away," he said simply.

Angelique smiled her thanks. "But I can't be here all day, every day. I have to work for Maman. And then the flies will be in the wound. I should be helping Joseph with the smudge even now."

They looked at each other. "The smudge!" they said in unison. "It keeps the flies away from the meat," Angelique reasoned, "so maybe it will keep the flies away from Michif." Often the horses were tethered downwind of a smudge when the flies were bad. "I'll ask Papa."

As she walked him back, Angelique led Michif past the remaining buffalo carcasses. She was relieved to see that he didn't shy, although he did snort when he saw a buffalo head lying nearby.

Joseph was tending the smudge fire. For once he didn't complain about her not being around. Maman was helping him. Her mother didn't say anything, just put her arm around Angelique. For a while they worked quietly, turning the drying strips of meat. Soon it would be dry enough to start pounding into pemmican.

"Maman, François's *kokum* had a salve she put on Marie's father's wounds. Would that work for Michif?"

Her mother paused. "You could ask."

Angelique did not dare ask to leave. She had been away so much, leaving the work to others.

Her mother watched her fidget for a moment or two, then smiled. "Go, run and ask her."

Angelique was off, back to camp.

CHAPTER N.º 11

Marie's father lay in the shade of the tipi, but now it was Marie who smeared the sticky salve on his legs. It was hard to see if the wounds had improved, but the man was smiling fondly at his daughter between occasional painful grimaces.

Marie smiled up at her. "He is going to be well again."

"I am so happy." Angelique smiled back. "The salve is working?"

Again Marie's happy smile. "It is a miracle. François's *kokum* says there might not even be big scars." She looked at the half-empty container and pursed her lips. "We must hope, though, that no one else is injured, for we have had to use almost all her supply."

Angelique fought back the tears. How could she possibly ask to use some for Michif when one of the hunters might need it?

She turned blindly around the tipi and nearly ran into the old medicine woman.

"What is it you want, little one?" she asked, not unkindly.

"Please," Angelique stammered, "the salve . . . I need to know what that is."

The woman smiled a little. "Spruce gum," she said. "It stops the bleeding and protects the wounds so that they can heal." She turned away. "I only hope I have enough . . . not many spruce trees on the prairie."

No, Angelique thought, *but I saw some little spruce trees. Where? When? It was somewhere near water, not long ago.* If only she could remember. She turned, nearly bumping into François, who had been standing behind her—how long she didn't know.

Angelique was glad to see her friend, even if she wished he wouldn't keep creeping up behind her. He'd done the same thing when she'd been watering Michif earlier that day, and she was getting sick of it. And then she remembered where she'd seen the little spruce trees. It had been when she'd gone upstream to water Michif. Suddenly, she wasn't a bit angry.

"François!" She really was glad to see him now. "I need a dish or something to scoop up some spruce gum."

"You're going to chew? Why not just put it in your mouth?"

Angelique laughed. It was true, they'd both tried chewing the bitter gum. "No . . . I need it to put on Michif. If it works for people, it should work for horses, don't you think?"

François found her a battered tin cup, and she tucked it under her arm. Together they slipped through camp, following the stream.

Yes, she was right! There, just beyond where

she'd watered Michif that morning, the stream widened and a small pool lay still and smooth. Beside it grew several small spruce trees. Now she wished she'd brought a knife to scrape the gum that hung like teardrops from breaks in the bark. She did the best she could with the cup.

"Use this." François pulled a blade from a leather sheath at his waist.

Angelique gasped. How long had he been wearing that? Boys did like to pretend they were grown up. She resisted the urge to scold him.

"It's very good that you brought that!" She smiled gratefully.

In no time, she had the cup over half full, and she turned to go.

"Wait!" François took the knife back and scraped bark away in several places on the two larger trees.

Angelique understood. Now, the trees would ooze more gum, and later they could come back and gather more for the medicine woman's work.

They skirted camp and ran silently out to where she'd left Michif tethered.

Joseph was still feeding the smudge with the buffalo chips they'd gathered. Michif paced restlessly back and forth, his tail swishing violently at the cloud of flies. The smudge didn't seem to be doing much good at all.

"Oooh, Michif! Look at you!"

The lashing tail had only sometimes managed to keep the flies away, and the wound was bleeding much more than it had been before. Angelique wiped away as much of the blood as she could and then quickly applied the spruce gum. When she'd finished, there was a great sticky patch on the horse's rump but no more blood, and the flies now seemed more interested in the blood smeared on Angelique's sleeve.

Her mother came over from where she had been turning the strips of meat. She looked at Michif and nodded, then she looked at Angelique.

"You'd better go and change and rinse that blouse in the stream. And . . ." she said, pointing to the cup, "you can clean *that* before someone wants some tea!"

The next few days were busy ones. The meat dried quickly in the hot, spring sunshine. Now the strips had to be pounded into pemmican. Dried meat was too bulky to take home.

This was work for the men. A new buffalo hide was hung from posts, three on each side, and the slabs of meat were thrown in. Angelique watched as Papa and François's father, one at either end of the hide, whacked away at the meat with sticks, pounding it to a pulp.

Last year, at the fall hunt, they'd picked and

dried saskatoon berries, and those had been added too, but there were no berries now.

Angelique was keeping Michif tethered on the rise nearby so that she could watch him. As often as she could she would untie his tether rope and exercise him, so that his injured hindquarter didn't stiffen up.

"Angelique!" Papa called. "Ask Maman if the grease is ready."

She ran to her mother, who was stirring chunks of fat in a large black cast-iron pot over the fire. When these had melted, the liquid fat would be mixed in with the meat.

"It's ready now, but it's too heavy for you to carry with me . . . fetch your father, if you don't mind."

Angelique laughed. She didn't mind running back and forth one bit. It was a glorious morning, promising a hot afternoon. Luckily there was a fresh breeze. She wouldn't have wanted to be her mother, though, standing by the fire and stirring the sputtering fat. She supposed she ought to offer to help with that.

Papa saved her. "Why don't you and Joseph take Michif for some exercise. He needs to move more."

Angelique smiled happily. It was wonderful that Papa trusted her to look after the injured horse. *Why,* she thought, *I've been doing* all *the caring for Michif, moving his tether, and twice a day taking him upstream to drink.* At night she would bring Michif into the cart area that was encircled by their tipis. It was where the valuable horses were kept. Even though the others outside camp were guarded, horses were often stolen.

With Joseph at her side, Angelique ran with Michif. As always, running free across the prairie made her feel that if she let go of the halter shank she might just float away and drift, cloud-like, in the vastness of the sky.

"Angelique," Joseph panted beside her, "why don't we ride Michif? I'm sure that if we asked Papa he'd let us, now that Michif's not—"

"*No!*" Angelique couldn't let him finish. She

slowed the horse to a walk and glared at Joseph. "No! We won't ask Papa and we *won't* ride Michif!"

Even as she spoke she realized that she was not really angry with Joseph for his question. She was afraid. If Papa said yes, they could ride, it would mean that he didn't believe that Michif would be a buffalo runner again. Was that why Papa was avoiding the horse, letting her take care of him? She had hoped it was because he knew it made her happy, but maybe there was another reason. The loss of a trained buffalo runner was a disaster for a family, but was there more? What had happened to the bond between man and horse?

Her joy in the day faded, and they walked the horse back in silence.

Maman was sewing up the hide full of meat with sinew. The hairy side of the hide was turned out, and inside the pemmican would stay dry and safe on the trip back. No rain or dust could penetrate. She watched as one of the other men helped Papa lift it into the cart. A hide full of meat and grease was very heavy; even two men together struggled to heave it high enough. She waited until they'd finished.

"Papa?" She wasn't sure how to begin, but he looked kindly down at her.

". . . About Michif . . ." Was it her imagination, or had his eyes dimmed at the sound of the horse's name? Was it some of the sadness of the day the horse was injured, or something else—defeat? Angelique didn't want to think about it. She fumbled on, wishing she could think of the words that needed to be said. "He's not limping, he's running really well, and the wound looks as if it's healing and not sore, and . . ." She couldn't look at her father's eyes any more. "Perhaps . . . you could ride him . . . a little?"

She was glad he turned away so she wouldn't have to face him. "Not yet . . . maybe some time . . . not yet . . ." he said, and he walked away.

CHAPTER N.º 13

There was dancing that night. There had been dancing every night. Part of the fun of the hunt was getting to know people from other communities who had joined them as the cartloads of families headed south to find the buffalo.

Joseph was busy playing with some new friends creeping under the carts. Screams of laughter as they chased one another almost blended with Jean's fiddle music.

Angelique had made a new friend too, Marie Letendre. They'd even danced together, circling with the other girls, trying to copy the dance steps. They'd laughed more than they'd danced, stumbling over one another's feet. But tonight she didn't want to join the others. Tonight she stood alone.

The most wonderful thing in the world, she thought, would be to be able to ride Michif. She loved the horse, and if he didn't love her back he came as close to it as he did with anyone. Sometimes she had imagined herself on his back when she watched her father riding, racing, or training him.

But it was Michif's destiny to be the best of horses, a buffalo runner. And now she had ruined that. Except she didn't believe it. There was no limp. Today Michif had run with her just as he had before. She was sure that if her father would just ride him again, it would be as if nothing had ever happened. She was sure Michif was still brave.

She had been so wrapped in her thoughts that she hadn't noticed her father coming towards her until he was nearly in front of her, his hand outstretched.

*The steps weren't hard, and
the rhythm of the fiddle tunes
made you step lively.*

"Come!" he said. "Dance with your old Papa!"

She laughed then. They'd always had a dance or two at other hunts and at home at the winter parties. She remembered that not too long ago, when she'd been not much younger than Joseph, he'd still picked her up to dance. She took his hand and followed him back.

Watching the dancing and practising with her friends had helped. The steps weren't hard, and the rhythm of the fiddle tunes made you step lively. The trick was to keep moving. Soon she was spinning breathlessly, trying to keep up to Papa and not get trampled by the other dancers.

"Thank you!" he said with a little bow when the dance was over.

She turned to walk away, but her father held her hand to keep her with him. This time the look in his eyes was as it used to be. "And thank you for all your good care of Michif. I looked. The wound is healing better than I ever thought it could. You must have the touch."

This time her tears were from happiness, and she stood alone because she wanted to savour the joy.

The next morning, Angelique helped her mother pack up the tipi and tie the poles onto the top of the cart ready to go home. The heavily laden carts screeched and groaned as the long procession set out. Nobody but the very old or very young would be riding in the carts now. She wasn't looking forward to all the dust and noise, but once the carts were moving it would be better. She and Joseph would be riding on his pony. Maybe they could get the lazy thing to gallop ahead and get away from the dust.

The hunt was over, and it had been a good one. Lots of good food to eat and pemmican for themselves, and to share or sell. Marie's father seemed to be much better and was hobbling around. And the Larocques had a new baby, come early to surprise everyone.

But the best part was that she could see her father mounting Michif, the horse dancing, eager to be off.

Her mother came up beside her and echoed Angelique's thoughts.

"It will be all right! You'll see . . ." Her mother's arm was around Angelique's shoulder. "And by the time we are ready for the fall hunt . . . who knows?"

Angelique smiled. It would be all right.

Dear Reader,

Did you enjoy reading this Our Canadian Girl adventure? Write us and tell us what you think! We'd love to hear about your favourite parts, which characters you like best, and even whom else you'd like to see stories about. Maybe you'd like to read an adventure with one of Our Canadian Girls that happened in your hometown—fifty, a hundred years ago or more!

Send your letters to:

Our Canadian Girl

c/o Penguin Canada

10 Alcorn Avenue, Suite 300

Toronto, ON M4V 3B2

Be sure to check your bookstore for more books in the Our Canadian Girl series. There are some ready for you right now, and more are on their way.

We look forward to hearing from you!

Sincerely,

Barbara Berson

PENGUIN BOOKS CANADA

P.S. Don't forget to visit us online at www.ourcanadiangirl.ca—there are some other girls you should meet!

Canada's

1608
Samuel de
Champlain
establishes
the first
fortified
trading post
at Quebec.

1759
The British
defeat the
French in
the Battle
of the
Plains of
Abraham.

1812
The United
States
declares war
against
Canada.

1845
The expedition of
Sir John Franklin
to the Arctic ends
when the ship is
frozen in the pack
ice; the fate of its
crew remains a
mystery.

1869
Louis Riel
leads his
Metis
followers in
the Red
River
Rebellion.

1871
British
Columbia
joins
Canada.

1755
The British
expel the
entire French
population
of Acadia
(today's
Maritime
provinces),
sending
them into
exile.

1776
The 13
Colonies
revolt
against
Britain, and
the Loyalists
flee to
Canada.

1837
Calling for
responsible
government, the
Patriotes, following
Louis-Joseph
Papineau, rebel in
Lower Canada;
William Lyon
Mackenzie leads the
uprising in Upper
Canada.

1867
New
Brunswick,
Nova Scotia,
and the United
Province of
Canada come
together in
Confederation
to form the
Dominion of
Canada.

1870
Manitoba joins
Canada. The
Northwest
Territories
become an
official
territory of
Canada.

1762
Elizabeth

Timeline

1885
At Craigellachie, British Columbia, the last spike is driven to complete the building of the Canadian Pacific Railway.

1898
The Yukon Territory becomes an official territory of Canada.

1914
Britain declares war on Germany, and Canada, because of its ties to Britain, is at war too.

1918
As a result of the Wartime Elections Act, the women of Canada are given the right to vote in federal elections.

1945
World War II ends conclusively with the dropping of atomic bombs on Hiroshima and Nagasaki, Japan.

1873
Prince Edward Island joins Canada.

1896
Gold is discovered on Bonanza Creek, a tributary of the Klondike River.

1905
Alberta and Saskatchewan join Canada.

1917
In the Halifax harbour, two ships collide, causing an explosion that leaves more than 1,600 dead and 9,000 injured.

1939
Canada declares war on Germany seven days after war is declared by Britain and France.

1949
Newfoundland, under the leadership of Joey Smallwood, joins Canada.

1896
Emily

1865
Angelique

1917
Penelope

Don't miss your chance to meet all the girls in the Our Canadian Girl series...

The story takes place in Montreal, during the smallpox epidemic of 1885. Marie-Claire, who lives in a humble home with her working-class family, must struggle to persevere through the illness of her cousin Lucille and the work-related injury of her father – even to endure the death of a loved one. All the while, Marie-Claire holds out hope for the future.

The year is 1917. Penny and her little sisters, Emily and Maggie, live with their father in a small house in Halifax. On the morning of December 6, Penny's father is at work, leaving Penny to get her sisters ready for the day. It is then that a catastrophic explosion rocks Halifax.

Ten-year-old Rachel arrives in northern Nova Scotia in 1783 with her mother, where they reunite with Rachel's stepfather after escaping slavery in South Carolina. Their joy at gaining freedom in a safe new home is dashed when they arrive, for the land they are given is barren and they don't have enough to eat. How will they survive?

Watch for more Canadian girls coming soon and visit the website at www.ourcanadiangirl.ca

Don't miss your chance to meet all the girls in the Our Canadian Girl series...

It's 1896 and Emily lives a middle-class life in Victoria, B.C., with her parents and two little sisters. She becomes friends with Hing, the family's Chinese servant and, through that relationship, discovers the secret world of Victoria's Chinatown. She also begins to understand the disparity between those like herself who have much, and those, like Hing and the family he left behind in China, who have little.

It's 1939 and times are tough in Vancouver. Ellen's dad has just lost his job and Ellen and her family have to move across town to stay with he grandfather. Ellen feels so lonely in her new home, and the neighbourhood around her feels unfamiliar. It is not until Ellen meets a new friend and discovers there are people who are much worse off than her that she will learn the true meaning of generosity.

In December of 1940 on the South Shore of Nova Scotia, Izzie Morash, her brother and their friends prepare for a very special Christmas. Despite wartime rationing, and the infrequency of winter visits, the Morash grandparents, aunt, uncle and cousins are coming for Christmas. But plans go awry two days before Christmas, when a huge storm hits the village. Can Izzie figure out a way to save Christmas for everyone?

Watch for more Canadian girls coming soon and visit the website at www.ourcanadiangirl.ca

Check out the
Our Canadian Girl website

Fun Stuff

- E-cards
- Prizes
- Activities
- Poll

Fan Area

- Guest Book
- Photo Gallery
- Downloadable *Our Canadian Girl* Tea Party Kit

Features on the girls and more!

www.ourcanadiangirl.ca